I0719680

Beneath the Sun

Beneath the Sun

Ricky Allen

COPYRIGHT

Beneath the Sun is a work of fiction. The names, characters, businesses, places, events, incidents and dialogue are drawn from the author's imagination and are not to be construed as real. Any resemblance to actual events or persons, living or dead, is entirely coincidental.

Printed in the United States of America.

First Printing, 2018

ISBN-9781947656734

The Butterfly Typeface Publishing

PO BOX 56193 Little Rock Arkansas 72215

www.butterflytypeface.com

butterflytypeface.imw@gmail.com

BENEATH THE SUN CONTENTS

DEDICATION

... to Redemptive Love

x

FOREWORD

In *Beneath the Sun*, author Ricky Allen, will take you on a rich journey. Not just through the cobblestone streets, colorful souks, and beautiful sights of Morocco, but you will go on a journey to and through love. It's a path he knows well. From the early years of life (which were filled with the unconditional and indomitable love of his fiercely strong and beautiful grandmother and mother) to the contours of manhood, faith, relationships, and fatherhood, Ricky Allen knows love.

This book is long overdue in many ways because it's been flourishing under wraps in his life and creative space for decades. Over the years, I've seen glimpses of Redo and Beatrice's story, and I'm glad my dad has taken the time to pen this beautiful book. Part memoir and part illustrative fiction, *Beneath the Sun*, will leave you inspired and encouraged to stay on the journey to and through love. I have been walking that road with Ricky Allen for 30+ years, and I have learned far more from him than a foreword can hold.

Take a moment to savor the wisdom within these pages. May *Beneath the Sun* be a blessing as you write your own love story.

--Rhonda Ford

ACKNOWLEDGMENT

God is Love!

Because He is Love, He does all things in Love. He demonstrated the greatness of His character by unselfishly giving all of Himself for the object of His love.

Through the richness of His mercy and the openness of His grace, He invites us to experience and instructs us to share the divine nature of Love.

Love covers a host of blunders.

Love is patient and kind.

Love is not envious, boastful, or rude.

Love does not demand its own way.

Love is not irritable.

Love doesn't keep score of wrongdoing.

Loves is not happy about injustice.

Love is happy whenever truth abounds.

Love never gives up.

Love never loses faith.

Love is always hopeful.

Love endures trying circumstance.

Love is a more excellent way.

Love is the greatest of all gifts.

Love abides forever.

From childhood until now, I've spent countless hours dreaming and pantomiming a life with love.

Love had kept me from perils seen and unseen when the odds were seemingly stacked against me.

Love has inspired me during times of self-doubt and uncertainty.

Love has restored hope and happiness in living.

Love has released its miraculous influence on me, in me and through me.

There is a season for everything and a time to every purpose under the Heavens.

Now is a time to love!

Love is waiting for you to "Show up."

--Ricky Allen

A WORD FROM THE PUBLISHER

I love this book.

Beneath the Sun has opened my eyes to the things I thought I knew about love and relationships.

For me, the overwhelming theme of *Beneath the Sun* is not only redemptive love, but learning how to navigate such a love. An extraordinary love requires extraordinary care.

Most of what we've been taught and shown about love is not what is presented in this book. We see Redo and Beatrice exercise restraint, caution, and reverence for love. We have been conditioned to believe that love hurts, that it should be reciprocal, and that it is more about physicality.

Nothing can be further from the truth.

Loving is not about what you receive, but is about what you are prepared to give. It is not about what you seek, but about opportunities that find you.

The Bible teaches us what love is (patient, kind, protects, trusts, hopes, never fails, etc...) **1 Corinthians 13:4-8**, but for various reasons, we have chosen to ignore God's instruction and description of love.

Beneath the Sun is a loving, honest, and entertaining depiction of what love looks like from a spiritual aspect.

If you know that we're spiritual beings having a physical experience, you can appreciate the fact that love should not be limited to what we feel, but rather reconciled back to what we know.

Remember, among other things, love is patient. Love is kind. Love trusts, hopes, and never fails.

I challenge you to question what you feel. Ask yourself how do your feelings 'match up' with what you know.

Don't just read *Beneath the Sun*, study it and learn from it. When you're done, I challenge you to reconsider what you thought you knew.

What I've come to know is this: without coercion, expectation, or obligation, love will find its way ... right where you are.

--Iris M. Williams

Author/Publisher

PROLOGUE

AWAKENED

It's 6:00 AM, Monday Morning at the Le Royal Mansour. I hear the birds singing. As I slowly drag out of bed due to the long flight and sleepless night, I am drawn to the light piercing through my window.

I make a fresh cup of coffee and walk out onto the balcony. I am taken by the beauty of butterflies glistening as they flutter in the sun and gently land upon the Roses of Sharon in the well-manicured indoor courtyard.

Is this just a prefigure to what awaits me, I wonder, great cities, vast deserts and picturesque coastlines? I've got twelve days to soak it all in…

I purposed this trip to be one of relaxation from my busy life back in the States. As a single professional, working for a Fortune 500 Corporation and a clergyman with pastoral duties, seldom have I taken time for just me. I was alone and had nothing and no one to serve, but me. It was a time for me to re-center and reconnect.

Twelve Days.

Seven Different Places.

Moments that would change my life.

ONE

Casablanca [kas-uh-blang-kuh]

NOWHERE TO BE

What a way to start a day! The birds chirping taking up the silent spaces in the air, and the butterflies are everywhere, around the trees and fluttering past me. I have nowhere to be and plenty of time to get there.

My original plan was to get up, rent a car and explore the city on my own. However, I soon realized that there was so much to see. I didn't know where to start. Expectantly, I went down for breakfast and indulged in my favorites, warm sweet pancakes, scrambled eggs with cheese, hash browns, hot steaming coffee and a small glass of ruby red grapefruit juice. After breakfast, I decided I needed to walk it off so; I stopped by the concierge desk and asked for a map.

I make my way over to the front desk and see a tall man with dark hair and a slim build. He looks up and smiles when he sees me coming. I scanned his name tag and greeted him as if I already knew him.

"Hello, Victor!"

"Hello Monsieur," he said as he extended his hand. His French accent was thick and strong but easy to understand.

"Redo Stuart," I said as I extended my hand in return.

"Hello, Mr. Stuart. How did you sleep?" He asked.

"Like a rock," I replied while popping my neck and rolling my shoulders outward. "Oh my, that felt good."

Victor laughed. "I didn't know rocks slept."

"They don't," I said. "They sink. And that's exactly what I did." I rolled my neck around again trying to loosen the tight muscles. "When my head hit that pillow, I sank into unconsciousness."

We both laughed.

"What are your plans for the day, Mr. Stuart?"

"Victor, you can call me Redo."

Victor relaxed after I told him to call me by my name. "Merci beaucoup, Monsieur Redo."

"De rein," I responded.

Victor looked at me smiling; his eyes crinkled

with a sense of delight from my French response.

Before leaving Arizona, I had spent a little time familiarizing myself with some French greetings and the proper responses. It felt good exchanging words with Victor in French; however, I knew my limitations.

"What are my plans for the day?" I repeated. "Well, Victor, I thought I would walk around a bit, rent a car and do a little site seeing."

Victor's brows furrowed in curiosity. "Is this your first trip to Morocco," he asked. "What brings you here?"

"Yes, it is my first trip to Morocco. It just sounded like a fun place to visit. I wanted to experience a different culture."

"Monsieur Redo, might I suggest a full tour of the Moroccan region? I have just the guided tour in mind, and there happens to be one more open slot. The bus leaves at 12:00 noon. I can get you on it if you are flexible," he said with a raised eyebrow.

I took the challenge. "Victor, I've got twelve days to flex, tell me more…"

According to Victor, Casablanca would be the

first stop on the tour. It is the largest city in Morocco. A large city was the very thing I was trying to escape. I wanted a more quiet and cozy setting in which to unwind and relax. Yet, despite the tours fast pace and daily schedules, I found myself eager to participate.

Noon quickly arrived. I hated to leave the comforts of the Le Royal Mansour and the gentle cool breeze of the Atlantic Ocean. However, I was excited as I boarded the 25-passenger tour bus.

As we rode through the whitewashed Moorish buildings that extended from the coast, I appreciated the interesting mixture of tower blocks and French colonial architecture. I slowly began to unwind and embrace the tour.

The tour guide announced, "The itinerary for the day is a visit to the Hassan II Mosque and the local souks (marketplaces)."

I hadn't done much research on Morocco and hadn't a clue as to what to expect. Heedlessly, I was entirely open to new discoveries.

The Hassan II Mosque was one of just two mosques in the country that's open to non-Muslims. The mosaics, marble columns, horseshoe-shaped arches and carved, painted wooden ceilings are breathtaking.

I found the souks interesting; the mouthwatering local food to try, handicrafts from leather bags to brightly painted pottery and large bowls of olives, were all intense.

I was amused watching as trading caravans gathered and sold their goods. Not only are the souks marketplaces, but they also serve as cultural centers where many celebrations and festivals are held.

The vibrant colors of people, buildings and merchandise are so atmospheric.

I slowly exhale as I take it all in.

TWO

Rabat [rah-baht]

SUDDENLY

It's 7:00 PM. The moonlit glow, fifty-seven-mile drive along the Northern Atlantic coast was spectacular! I could smell the sweet and relaxing citrus of the orange groves as we drove in route to The Villa Mandarine Hotel. It has been a long day. I'm ready for bed.

I entered the hotel with my feet dragging beneath me. The heels of my shoes clicked with each step I took. The oak of the front desk was dark and smooth to the touch; everything about this place was relaxing. The clerk at the desk looked up at me with a warm-hearted smile.

"Good evening Monsieur."

"Good evening," I replied, placing my hands on the desk for support.

"May I have your name please?"

"Redo Stuart," I nodded to him and straightened up my posture.

"We have your room ready Monsieur Stuart."

"Thank you," I said, tired and ready to unwind.

As I waited for him to check me in, I glanced through the brochure on the desk admiring the hotel amenities. The rooms featured a pleasant seating area with an LCD TV and a welcoming couch. There is also a private balcony with views of the garden. I took a moment and imagined myself out on the balcony in the morning, sipping my coffee and taking in the light breeze and the early sunrise.

"Here you are," he said pulling me out of my thoughts. "You will be in room 913. The elevators are down the hall, to the left."

I nodded, grabbed my bags and up to the room I went. *Room 913, my room.*

I swiped the key. As a long day would have it, the door wouldn't unlock. I tried a second and third time. Still, the door wouldn't open. All I got was the red blinking light in my face denying me accesses to the room and my long-awaited sleep. Back to the lobby, I go.

I turn the corner of the elevator and see the clerk with the same smile.

"How's your room, Monsieur Stuart?"

"Well, I don't know," I said attempting to remain pleasant in spite of the aggravation. "My key wouldn't work."

His smile faded. "My apologies," he offered. "Let me take care of that for you."

Suddenly she appeared, standing still as everything in the lobby seemingly rotated on an axis around her. Then she moved.

Taken by her graceful stride, I went blind and deaf for a moment.

"Monsieur, Monsieur… your key."

"I'm sorry," I said as I shook my head to regain consciousness.

"No problem," he said as he grinned and handed me my new key.

I made my way back to the room and was able to access it this time. The accommodations were nicely appointed as indicated in the brochure. Its contemporary styling was a canvas of white with accents of lemon yellow and lime green. It was a nice compliment to the calm spa-like surroundings. After a hot shower, I fell asleep effortlessly in the soft bed, the smooth cool sheets covering me.

The next morning, I rose early and enjoyed coffee on the balcony as I imagined. Then I went down for breakfast on the terrace which led into the gardens.

Man, this is great.

But that thought was interrupted by thoughts of being successful and single. I was single by choice. I was preparing for that woman God has prepared for me.

If I could count the times I'd heard, "You need a woman," and charged a dollar each time I'd heard it, I'd have enough to buy that new motorcycle I've been saving for. Members of matchmakers anonymous, family and friends, just didn't know when to stop.

"More coffee Monsieur," the ebullient waitress asked interrupting my intrusive thoughts.

"Yes, please."

This timely interruption helped me embrace the moment and refocus on the serene tranquility of my surroundings.

Today was a free day.

Pierre, the tour guide, informed us that Rabat

was not in the main lineup of Morocco's tourist attractions. However, he said this capital city was full of charm. The international flair and importance was signified by the presence of foreign embassies and dignitaries. The palm tree-lined boulevards were clean and relatively free of traffic. This was a welcomed relief from the traffic in Casablanca. Actually, it was a suitable day for walking.

Among the many interesting things to do, I decided to spend the day at Museum Mohamed VI of Modern and Contemporary Art. The vibrant paintings and eccentric statues were aspiring. I must say the Picasso and Out of Africa exhibits were among my favorites.

As I continued to revel in such creative genius, I notice something strikingly familiar. It was her. The woman I saw yesterday. She seemed quiet and reserved compared to everyone else in the gallery.

She seemed to appear out of nowhere, in her own space. She gazes intensely as she floats from one piece of art to the next.

I watched her as she smiled while writing in a brown leather-bound journal. The way she moved, wrote; everything about her was enchanting.

Who was she? Where did she come from? Even more, what was she writing?

Is it me?

Or, is this divine?

Is it real or just an aspect of my mind?

Does destiny find us at such a place, at such a time?

Why am I thinking in ways I've never thought?

Why am I feeling things I've never felt?

Could I have been Adam …and she had been Eve?

What is it about her that foments my curiosity?

Lost in a mental wonderland, I drew closer to her. She was so engrossed in a particular piece of art that she never saw me coming.

The art was an exquisite rendition of the sun with its 'bronze orange' rim surrounding various geometric shapes of all sizes and vibrant colors, neatly grouped in what appeared to be regions with transparent boundaries.

I leaned in towards her, "Excuse me."

She jumped as though she had touched an unnoticeable hot flame and grabbed her chest as if her heart was trying to escape. She took a breath and clutched her journal to herself.

"I'm sorry," I said. "I didn't mean to startle you. I couldn't help but notice you and your appreciation for this piece of art. Redo Stuart." I extended my hand.

She glanced at my hand and then me. "Beatrice Napal," she smiled softly and gave her hand to mine.

Something leaped inside me like ten-thousand startled pheasants springing up from the bushes of a hunted field. Goosebumps traced my arms and my eyes widened.

What is this? I thought.

Suddenly, I felt alive!

THREE

Fez

A PIECE OF HEAVEN

It's day three, and the ride from Rabat to Fez was 125 miles, as the crow flies. Over three hours on the same tour bus and yet no sight of her. I couldn't get her off my mind.

What brought her to Morocco? Was she traveling alone? Was she married, engaged or dating?

The day in Fez was enjoyable. The car-free zones were great for pedestrians weaving in and out of the busy souks. This city has been called the "Mecca of the West" and the "Athens of Africa."

There is an ambiance that suggests, *no man should be here alone without a woman to love.* Not just any woman but the woman that was reserved just for him. That priceless jewel embedded in the crown of his manhood. Yet, here I was like a Prince with a crown and no jewel.

On my way back to the hotel, Palais Amani, I stopped by the quaint Café Clock with its small tables and sofas for patrons to sit and relax while surfing the Internet or talking to someone. I enjoyed my mint green tea and free WI-FI. I had intentions on leaving work behind, however, here I was reconnecting and checking on things back in Glendale.

The sounds of traditional Moroccan music reminded me that I was not here on a job assignment or mission trip. I look around at the people who had detached themselves from the world outside these walls. I disconnected from the Wi-Fi and decided to make my way back to the hotel. I walked at a steady pace to enjoy my surroundings. The woman, Beatrice kept appearing in my mind.

Where did she come from?

Did she come here alone?

As I entered the hotel lobby, I recognized a few people from the tour bus. But still, no sight of her.

Palais Amani, located near the Golden Triangle in the ancient medina is opulent. It has refined dining and spacious accommodation. From what I learned on the ride here, the place also has a salon, library, a rooftop bar, extensive terraces, and a traditional Turkish Bath and spa. It is the perfect place for relaxing.

Before heading up to my room for a shower, I

decided to stop by the concierge desk to inquire about any scheduled activities for the night.

This place is wonderful, I thought. *There is no need for me to explore the city tonight when I can be just as well entertained here.*

"Good Afternoon," I greet the concierge.

"Good Afternoon Sir. How may I help you?"

"You can help me have a wonderful evening," I say playfully. "Any suggestions?"

"For a wonderful evening, Sir, I suggest dinner at our main restaurant, Eden, here at Palais Amani and then dancing on the rooftop terrace." He gave me the perfect employee smile that I have been presented at every hotel since I arrived in Morocco.

I drummed my fingers on the desk and gave him a flat smile. "Thank you for the suggestions," I said.

Now I was painfully aware that I had neither a dinner or dancing partner. I had been perfectly fine coming on this trip alone. I've repeatedly told myself that my life is too busy and complicated for casual dating.

The wind was warm and soft. The crescent moon smiled as the stars sang together, a melody of sweet existence. Rhythms of contentment made my body sway as I lounged on the terrace near the pool. The sights and sounds of the fountains were bright and defined; nothing missed my gaze.

I knew Eden at Palais Amani would be opening for dinner in an hour.

As I took in the panoramic view of the terrace and the pool, I saw Beatrice head in my direction. Once again, something stirred inside me. This time it is was more like the soft fluttering of butterfly wings. Now, my arms felt a bit warm and clammy.

I've seen her three times, I thought. *How can I make this third time a charm?*

As I contemplated, Beatrice stopped at a nearby bar. I could hear her ask for a glass of spring water. She then gracefully sauntered to the edge of the rooftop terrace and propped her elbows on the mosaic wall. Her hair was pulled to the side. The beautiful red dress danced as the warm, soft wind blew. The moonlit sky and bright stars put a spotlight on her, giving a halo effect around her hair. At this moment, she's all I could see.

I got up and began to walk in her direction, hoping she would stand still long enough for me to speak to her.

"How's the view?" I asked.

Once again, she jumped.

"Ms, Mrs. Napal, right?" I once again extended my hand. I could see the curious look in her eye. "Redo Stuart," I said. "We briefly met at the Museum Mohamed VI of Modern and Contemporary Art."

She seemed slightly surprised that I would remember her name and nodded while saying, "Yes, yes, nice to see you again." Then she smiled and said, "The view is breathtaking, Mr. Stuart."

"You can call me Redo," I said.

She replied, "And you can call me Beatrice." She relaxed back into the position she was in before I approached her.

The view is indeed breathtaking! And I wasn't referring to Morocco. Up close I got a better look at her. She had gentle eyes and an elegant frame.

"What brings you to Morocco Beatrice?"

She looked at me and said, "I had a generous friend who won an all-expense paid trip to

Morocco; however, she couldn't make it. She insisted that I take the trip since she couldn't. Otherwise, it would be lost."

"Wow, that's some friend you have," I said.

"Yes, the only thing she asked of me, was to keep a daily journal of my experiences and to share them with her when I return home." She turned back towards me, seeming interested in what I have to say. "What about you Redo? What brought you to Morocco?"

"I needed a vacation," I said simply. "Morocco sounded like an interesting place. I'm glad I made this choice." I leaned against the mosaic wall with her wanting to keep the conversation going.

She quietly smiled back and said, "I'm glad I was given this opportunity."

"Beatrice, I have a dinner reservation tonight here in the hotel's restaurant, Eden at Palais Amani, in five minutes. Would you like to join me?" She looked a little taken back, shocked at my invitation.

"Well-," she began.

"I'm sorry," I said suddenly aware of my bold

request. "I understand if this is a bit rash."

"No, no," she protested, holding her hands out in defense. Looking concerned that she might have hurt my feelings, she explain, "I planned to eat; I just didn't know where."

"So, is that a yes?" I asked.

She took a second, "Yes," she smiled and straightened up from her once leaning position. "I will join you for dinner."

Keeping in time with our steps, we made our way to the elevators and found the restaurant.

"Good evening," I greeted the attendant. "I have a reservation for Redo Stuart."

The restaurant host said, "Yes, Mr. Stuart, right this way. We are ready to scat you."

As we sat, I couldn't help but notice the live music playing. It was easy listening.

"Is this okay?" I asked.

"It's great," she said. "Would you excuse me?" She asked as she began to rise from her chair.

I said, "Sure," and rose to pull out her chair.

"No need," she said.

"I know. Allow me."

When she returned, I rose again to assist with her chair. She looked perplexed. The attendant came and took our drink orders.

"Does anything on the menu interest you?"

"It's all interesting," she said, with eyes as bright as a 'deer in headlights.'

I laughed and replied, "Yes, when in Morocco, eat as the Moroccans."

"I think I'll have this." She turned the menu to me, pointed to the menu items with words consisting mostly of consonants and accents. Thankfully, the descriptions were helpful.

The attendant returned with the water, "Have you decided on a menu item to include in your dining pleasure?"

Interesting choice of words, I thought. *Did he somehow know that the food was of little interest to me at this very moment?* I wanted to know more about her.

I said while pointing to the menu, "The lady will have, BASSTILA FASSIA DJAJ OU LOUZ," (which was a traditional light pastry filled with Chicken and almonds, dusted in icing sugar and cinnamon).

The attendant replied, "excellent choix, belle femme."

I will have, POISSON DU JOUR, (which was a marinated filet of fish served with cracked wheat risotto and sautéed green vegetables)."

I looked up from the menu in time to catch her gazing at me before she sweetly offered, "I'm impressed."

"At what?" I asked.

"Are you always this nice?" She asked, without answering my question?

"I try," I replied, attempting to subdue my confidence.

She continued to smile, looked at me intently and said, "A woman could get used to this."

I returned the gaze and responded, "Really? Well, you've got nine days if you'd like to try."

"You are so eager," she said with a chuckle. "What do you do for a living?"

"I am bi-vocational," I replied.

"Bi-vocational; what exactly does that mean?" She leaned forward ready to listen to what I am about to tell her.

"I work as the Director of Corporate Communication and Internal Affairs, for a Hospitality Group in Glendale, Arizona. I'm also an Associate Pastor at New Hope Christian Fellowship, also in Glendale Arizona."

She nodded in curiosity once I told her all I did for work.

"What about you Beatrice? What do you do for a living?"

She sat back in her chair, "I am an International Art Curator, currently assigned to our Paris, France office. However, in my spare time, I teach creative writing at The American University of Paris."

My heart sank, *Paris, that's far.* I knew I needed to lighten the mood, so I decided to joke with her. "Looks like you are bi-vocational as well," I said in an attempt to be funny, hoping she'd laugh.

"I guess so, Redo."

She did, with her sweet smile. I couldn't help but smile back at her.

As we continued talking about our lives in Arizona and Paris, the attendant returned with dinner. The presentation was masterful. We mutually agreed that the entrées were mouthwatering.

Now, if she would only agree to join me on the rooftop terrace for music and maybe to dance, I thought.

We ended the dinner with coffee, CHOCOLAT (which was a rich and creamy chocolate mousse), and plenty of conversation and laughter.

As we exited the restaurant, I looked upwards at the sky then looked at her and said, "Beatrice, thanks for joining me for dinner. It was delightful."

"Thanks for inviting me," she said breathlessly. "I had a great time."

I thought, *the concierge suggestion for dinner and dancing were both a fantastic idea for an evening. Should I call it a night and settle for delightful? Or, do I go for wonderful and invite her to join me for music and dancing on the rooftop terrace?*

I went for wonderful.

"Beatrice, the concierge informed me that there are live music and dancing on the rooftop terrace. I thought it sounded like a wonderful way to end an evening. Once again, would you care to join me?"

"It's been a while since I've gone dancing," she said folding her arms down over herself holding her bag. "I love music and would be happy to join you."

"Awesome," I said.

After going back to our rooms to change into clothes suited for dancing, we met up on the rooftop terrace near the fountains.

The silver, calf-length dress was just as stunning as the red dress she wore for dinner. The reflection of the stars bounced off it like sparkling diamonds.

We sat and acclimated ourselves to the Moroccan beats. The music was a fusion of Arabic, Latin, Jazz, Rap, and Reggae. It was mystical and somewhat sensual. You have to feel this music in order to dance to it. My head, neck, and shoulders felt it. My mind was seeing it happen. Finally, I was ready.

"Beatrice, would you like to dance?"

"I'd love to," she agreed.

"I don't know how it will look," I warned her. "But judging by my head, neck, and shoulders, I can tear a dance floor up. However, I don't know if all that will work with my feet."

Simultaneously, we laughed.

"As long as we have fun, that's all that matters right?"

I nodded in agreement.

I got up, offered my hand as she playfully drew near me. I forgot all about my feet as we moved in response to the Moroccan beat.

Was it the Salsa? Was I even moving? Was this real or just in my head?

The driving percussions, the flirtatious oriental string, and the enchanting sounds drew us closer together.

I was in the moment.

We were dancing as one.

Tonight, was a night to remember!

It was a blissful piece of heaven.

FOUR

Erg Chebbi

OASIS

I awoke early the next morning in preparation for the next point of interest, Erg Chebbi.

I took a few extra moments to savor the memories of last night. They were wonderful! I caught myself smiling as I relived the aftershock of the pounding Moroccan beats, the conversation and dancing with Beatrice.

It felt as though the evening stood still and moved at warped speed, all at the same time, while simultaneously, we talked and danced. She was reserved but enchanting. It was paradoxical. With every thought, Beatrice's laugh echoed in my mind. For the first time, I can't imagine how it could have gone better. We connected in a way, unlike anything I'd experienced.

The drive to Erg Chebbi is ten hours, so, day four of the tour will be mostly traveling. Pierre met us in the lobby and covered some logistics for the day.

I didn't see Beatrice when we began boarding the bus. I proceeded down the aisle and took an aisle seat. This way, I figured I could see her when she boarded.

Strangely enough, between talking, laughing, and dancing, I didn't inquire whether or not she was making the entire tour. A gut retching feeling of regret came over me. I shut my eyes tightly wanting to go back to last night and ask.

Was last night the last time I would see her?

I glanced at my watch and realized the tour bus would be departing in ten minutes. I threw my head back, and closed my eyes to quiet my mind. Quickly, I dozed off to sleep. I felt a tap on my shoulder, and a sweet familiar voice ask, "Is the window seat taken?"

This time I jumped and gathered myself. As I looked up, there Beatrice stood.

"No, it's not taken, but it is reserved," I said with a slight grin. "Would you like to have this seat?"

"Only, if it's reserved for me," she replied with a raised eyebrow and that beautiful smile.

I stood and stepped aside for her to claim the window seat.

She started to scoot past me to take the seat. The scent of her perfume was invigorating. At first whiff, this fragrance seemed sweet and unassuming much like that of black currant and purple irises.

The scent took me back. Mom had a green thumb and grew various kinds of plants and herbs in our backyard. Often while playing in the heat of the day, I would chase loose balls into her flower and herb beds. As I stooped for the ball, I got a faint trace of the floral and herbal sugariness of those two kinds of plants in particular. It was enough for me to draw closer and explore the aromas more quietly.

As Beatrice wiggled to get comfortable in her seat, the scent lingered, and the sweetness transformed into something a little sultry and a little "naughty."

"How are you this morning?" I asked.

"I'm wonderful," Beatrice sweetly replied. "And, how are you?" She turned her head to look at me.

"I'm much better now." I pined with my answer to her. I felt relief fill my chest as she took her seat next to me.

"Is something wrong, Redo?" Beatrice asked concerned.

"No," I quickly replied. "At this moment, everything is right."

Beatrice settled into her seat and pulled out the leather-bound journal and began to write. I was curious about the nature of her writing but somehow managed to appear uninterested. I kept my eyes straight ahead, for the most part. Although, at times, I did glance at her.

Suddenly, she stopped writing and said, "Thanks again for a wonderful evening."

"Sure," I said smiling. "Thanks for joining me. It was the best time I've had in a while. And the company wasn't bad either."

Surprisingly, she said, "You are incredibly generous to invite me, and you're a smooth talker." She looked back to her journal smiling.

"No," I said soberly. "It really has been a while since I've spent an evening out doing something unrelated to work or church, especially, with a beautiful woman."

Beatrice looked back at me with her smile but also wide eyes with a new interest in what I was saying.

"I go to work, church and back home," I

continued. "Generally, my good time consists of taking a nice back-road ride through Sedona to the Grand Canyon and back to Glendale on my motorcycle."

She pauses for a second, thinking of what to say next.

"You don't look like the kind of guy that rides a motorcycle."

"What do you mean?" I sat back in my seat eager to hear her response.

"I mean, ah you, I ... never mind," she said recovering from a stumble. "What kind of motorcycle do you have?"

I could tell she felt terrible about her quick statement; it didn't offend me any. She shouldn't feel bad for it. She may think those who ride motorcycles wear leather jackets, have long scraggly beards, full sleeve tats on both arms or belong to a motorcycle gang. It was a stereotype for which I'd become accustomed.

"I have a Victory Cross Country. Do you know anything about bikes?"

"I know they are dangerous."

I laughed and said, "The bikes themselves have never harmed anyone."

"Touché," she said, as we both laughed. The unexpectedly awkward moment was erased by our laughter.

The thought of her living so far away from me came to my mind. "So, why did you settle in Paris France?"

She shrugged her shoulders, "I needed a change. I always dreamed of living in Paris. I had the perfect opportunity and took it."

"How long have you been there?"

"I've been there three years."

During, her pointed replies, I realized a shift in her voice tone and posture. Her tone became raw. Her posture became shielding.

I wanted to get more information about her. What can I say? My curiosity was taking over. "Where are you from? What drove the need for this change? Was it routine or a relationship gone bad?"

"Smooth talking, nosy and direct," she replied.

Clearly deflecting, Beatrice turned and looked

out the window. A few moments later, while yet staring out of the window, she continued, "I'm originally from St. Louis, Missouri. My experience has been that men don't stick around long if they don't get what they want. I want more than a convenient arrangement. So maybe the need for change was due to my weariness from such happenings."

She turned her head to look back at me. "I have the kind of job that can be done anywhere, and so when an opportunity to live abroad presented itself, I decided to take it. I decided it was time to reclaim my life and pursue my dream." Her posture straightened up in a matter of fact way.

As she spoke, I thought, *this is the perfect opportunity to not be in a convenient arrangement.*

Perhaps, Paris was a detour and not her destiny.

Beatrice turned from the window and said, "Enough about me. Tell me more about you."

"What would you like to know?"

"Whatever, you'd like to tell me," she said.

"Well, let me start by saying, I'm not one of those men who disappear if I don't get what I want. I don't want an arrangement."

I was hoping that my directness didn't come across as arrogance.

"Secondly, I'm sorry that you've had such unfortunate experiences with men."

She smiled lightly and nodded, processing what I told her.

We were four hours into the trip from Fez to Erg Chebbi. The effects of the late-night dancing and early morning conversation with Beatrice weighed heavily on my eyelids. After a time, I drifted off to sleep.

Pierre made a sudden swerve of the tour bus. The movement awakens me from my sleep only to find Beatrice's head comfortably resting against my shoulder. It was a beautiful sight; however, it didn't last long enough.

"I'm sorry," she said having been jolted by the erratic movement of the tour bus too and realizing that her head had found a resting place against my shoulder.

"It's okay," I said. "Were you comfortable?"

"I don't know. I was asleep," Beatrice teased as to submit a disclaimer for her head resting on my shoulder.

"Yes, I know you were asleep. I can tell by the drool on my shirt." We both laughed out loud, as she covered her mouth.

Beatrice was very lighthearted and had a good sense of humor. I enjoyed the playful banter.

Once again, she pulled out that leather-bound journal and began to write.

"Beautiful journal," I said.

"Thanks, I got it, especially for this trip. I promised my friend that I would capture as many memorable moments as possible."

I thought, *what memorable moment could she possibly have captured on the ride from Fez to Erg Chebbi?*

Finally, we arrive at one of the Erg Chebbi Luxury Desert Camps located in Merzouga. I was intrigued. The thing was that there was no parking lot or cars, just tents, sand, and camels. I was watching Beatrice's face for a reaction.

Nothing.

Wow, luxury living in the middle of a desert. "I haven't stayed in a tent since I was in the boy scouts," I said out loud.

"Did the boy scouts have luxury tents?" She asked whimsically.

I looked at her with a smile, knowing what I was about to say, wouldn't help. "No, but we had the finest earthly amenities," I said and laughed. "All the dirt, bugs, and bright stars a boy could ask for."

Her nose scrunched up when I said bugs.

We debarked and went to the 24-hour advisors' tent which only had room for a table and a chair. The staff was amiable and assured us that we were safe as they gave us our tent assignments and informed us of the planned seven o'clock barbecue dinner followed by a firework show.

This tent city is unlike anything I've ever seen.

The furnishings in my tent were remarkably beautiful as the hotel's furnishings in Casablanca Rabat and Fez. According to the hotel brochure, there were fifteen units.

As I settled into my tent, I wondered what was Beatrice thinking about all this.

Festivity time drew closer. I went out and sat under my portico. The tourists from our bus began to exit their tents. Beatrice exited her tent and walked down the flame-lit pathways. The amber lights extended from each tent to a central gathering place.

I walked over to Beatrice.

"How are your luxurious accommodations?" I asked.

I prepared for a smart response; however, she responded in reverie.

She beamed at me, "Unbelievable, the furnishings are wonderful. My worries were for nothing."

I thought so, too.

"We are luxury camping after all." We both laugh due to our previous conversation at first glance of the tents.

I looked out beyond the camp. I saw sand and lots of it. All the sand made me think of a story:

Legend has it when a wealthy family refused hospitality to a poor woman and her son, God, was offended and buried them under the mounds of sand called Erg Chebbi. All you see for miles here are sand dunes.

The barbecue, sounds of Moroccan music and fireworks display are greater than the 4th of July in the States.

Beatrice and I sat and didn't do much talking due to eating and taking in the backdrops. However, there was some nonverbal language that spoke loudly. We were enjoying sharing time and space in this place. It was an Oasis in the middle of the desert.

"Redo, I'm going to call it a night," Beatrice said breaking the silence. She started to get up from her seat and gather what things she had with her.

"Okay," I responded. Beatrice made her way down the lighted pathway to her tent. But, before she got too far, I shouted, "Hey! Tomorrow, I plan to go sand-dunning and to end the evening with a sunset camel ride. Would you like to join me?"

I make my way closer to her. *Am I too presumptuous?* I thought *as I waited for her answer?*

She looked at me eccentrically and said, "Sure, why not. What should I wear?"

I shrugged. "Shorts and a tee-shirt," I said with a smile. "And you might want to put on a cap. I'm sure you don't want to get sand in that beautiful hair."

"Funny," she said. "I don't have a cap."

"Don't worry," I said seriously. "I'll share mine. I don't have hair."

Laughing out loud, she looked at me and said, "You're something else Redo Stuart."

"Good night Beatrice, rest well. I'll meet you at the front desk in the morning at 7:00 AM."

As she turned and walked away, I couldn't help but wonder what she meant by, "You're something else." The way she said it and attached my full name was fetching.

The night is cool and pleasant. I wasn't ready to end the evening with Beatrice. As I lay in bed, my thoughts of being with her were abundant. I could hear her laugh faintly in my head. I could see her smile as the stars lit up her eyes. I could smell her sweet aroma. I could feel her head resting on my shoulders. I could taste…

How can I spend more time with her? I was thinking out loud. If only she could hear me from where she is. Did she feel what I felt? The nerves and curiosity of what she was thinking about kept my mind racing for answers.

I've done pretty well disconnecting from my electronic devices. But now, I needed some music. Right now, I'm not sure if I need to listen to *Jesus Keep Me Near the Cross or I Found Love.*

Either way, I was feeling strong about my feelings towards Beatrice and knew that I was falling for her.

I settled on some easy listening instrumentals. As the music played, my thoughts quieted.

As I drifted off to sleep, I thought, *do people really find love in mysterious ways? Or, is love at an appointed place and time awaiting their arrival?*

The sunrise greeted me as I walked out of my tent and headed towards the advisor's tent. Beatrice was already there.

She turned to me and greeted me with her nice smile. "Where's my cap?" She asked, holding out her hand waiting on an answer.

"What cap?" I asked, acting as if I didn't know what she was talking about.

For a moment, we played tug-of-war as I handed her my Victory Motorcycle ball cap. "Ready for the day?"

"As ready as I can be," she said with an iffy look on her face. I assumed she has never ridden a dune buggy before today.

We stopped by the outpost to rent a dune buggy and buy some sunscreen, an ice chest, water, snacks and a cap for my head. I didn't have to worry about getting sand in my hair, but the beaming sun would fry my scalp like an egg on a hot skillet if I didn't protect it.

We were off on an adventure together, and I could not wait. It was the first of its kind for both of us. I appreciated Beatrice's openness to try something new. I hope she wouldn't regret it.

As we dashed up and down the dunes, Beatrice was holding on for dear life and bellowing with laughter. She loved it, which made me feel a lot better. The impressive natural wonder of the orange hue Erg Chebbi dunes in the Sahara Desert was arresting, and Beatrice's laughter was infectious.

After pulling over for water and a snack, I asked Beatrice if she wanted to drive. To my surprise, she said yes.

"Oh, my!" I said. "Now it's my turn to sweat bullets and hold on for dear life."

Beatrice looked at me with a devious smile. "Oh

Redo, don't be so dramatic."

We both laughed as she drove off into the desert. She was cruising. The only time I ever really held on was when we went over hills. Beatrice drove as if she was drag racing down Whittier Blvd, in East L.A.

Once we stopped and got out, she complimented me on my driving as I complimented hers. "I think we both did well for the most part. We were driving over hills at a fast pace, of course, it was going to be bumpy." She smiled and made a good point.

Later, as Amad, the Camel Trekking Guide, prepared us for the hour and a half ride, I thought more about Beatrice's statement on the bus ride regarding men not staying around long if they don't get what they wanted. I wanted to know more about this heartbreak. I wanted to know her more. I knew I needed to find a time to ask but didn't want to be invasive.

Along the way, we stopped for group pictures. I also knew this was not the time for a personal conversation. I made light of my thoughts and focused on the moment.

"Beatrice, can I get a picture with you?" I stepped

towards her, thinking she wouldn't mind.

"I'm not good at taking pictures," she said waving her hand in refusal.

"You don't have to take it," I teased. "I'll take it. All you have to do is stand next to me and smile like you are enjoying it."

"You have an answer for everything." She shook her head and smiled.

Before she could strike the perfect pose, I took the perfect 'selfie.'

"Wait, I wasn't ready," She protested.

"Those are the best ones," I said. "Trust me."

"Trust you," she said locking her eyes onto mine in the most piercing way.

I felt as if she was looking into my soul.

"Yes, trust me."

Somehow, I knew neither of us was talking about a 'selfie' anymore.

Until now, the sublimely intense colors that blanket the horizon as the Sedona Arizona sun goes down were incomparable. I now have something to compare it too. The Moroccan sunsets are just as stunning. The intense glow of yellow and orange welcome you with open arms.

The camels moved slowly and gracefully through the desert as the golden sun quietly said goodnight.

As Amad leads the caravan back into camp, I could see the flicker from the campfire in the middle of the camp. I dismounted my camel and walked over to take Beatrice's hand as she dismounted. Once safely on the ground, she continued to hold my hand and didn't let go.

This day has been exhilarating and exhausting, I thought as we walked towards the campfire.

"Thanks for joining me."

"The pleasure was all mine," she said as the space between us decreased.

"Well, tomorrow, we'll be on the road again."

"Save me a seat," she said as she let go of my hand and walked down the pathway that led to her tent.

"I will."

FIVE

Mid Atlas Mountains

I FOUND LOVE

It's day six. I can't believe the time has gone so fast. I am looking forward to the five-hour ride from *Erg Chebbi* to *Ouarzazate.*

The morning birds are singing. The desert is sheen as this new day begins.

As I roll over and catch the sunlight leaking through the opening of my tent, my thoughts are of Beatrice. I can't help but think she's such an unlikely encounter. She is the woman of my dreams.

I had an interesting way of entertaining myself as a child. I played house. I pantomimed a life with *her. She* had no name. I can't tell you what *she* looked like or where *she* came from. I just knew *she* was mine and I was *hers. She* was in love, and I was in love.

After an early breakfast, Pierre greeted us as we boarded the bus. I claimed two mid-way seats and waited for Beatrice to join me.

When she finally made it onto the bus, I stood up. "Are you good with these seats?" I asked.

She smiled and started making her way into the row.

"These seats are fine."

As we begin our incline across the Middle Atlas Mountains, Beatrice began to write. I wondered how I could revisit her statement. Beatrice was reserved. Therefore, I didn't try to make much conversation.

I was enjoying the trip as we wound our way through the beautiful forests, jagged rock surfaces, and Berber villages.

Pierre was passionately telling us about his country, the landscapes and some of his favorite spots. As we crossed the Atlas Mountains range and began to descend deeper into the Sahara Desert, he stopped the bus to allow us to take pictures in front of the Atlas Mountains.

"Not only are these mountains rich in natural resources," Pierre boasts, "they are unparalleled in beauty."

I could see what he was talking about. The mountains had white tops with clouds dancing around the edges. Shades of green and brown adorned the sides. Waterfalls cascaded to its base.

I looked over at Beatrice who was admiring the mountains, as I admired her. "Up for another picture?" I asked to break the ice.

She looked at me and smiled. "Sure," she said. "This time wait until I'm ready."

"Okay," I agreed. "On three." I angled the camera at both of us with the Atlas Mountains in the background, taking up all the beauty in the sky. "How's that?" I asked, as I showed Beatrice the photo.

"I like it," she said, with a slight hint of excitement in her voice. "Airdrop me a copy?"

"Airdrop you a copy? What's that?"

Beatrice looked at me with suspicion and coached me through the process. Once the photo was dropped, we returned to the bus and got settled into our seats. Before Beatrice could become preoccupied; I took an opportunity to confess to her.

"I truly enjoy your presence, Beatrice. It took me the moment I first saw you. It was as if God dropped you straight from heaven."

"Is that the line you use on all your efforts to win a lady's heart?" She asked as she stared at me.

"No, I wouldn't waste yours or my time trying to *win* you. I didn't come to Morocco to *win* a woman's heart. I came to retreat from my busy life." I paused to take a breath. "Besides, I don't think twelve days is enough time to effectually, *win* someone's heart. You've found your way into my heart with unassertive effort."

She leaned away. "But, you don't know me," she said visibly upset by my declaration.

"But, I know love," I said, as I gently place my hand on hers.

She slowly removed her hand from under mine. "Redo, you are a nice guy. I appreciate the attention you've given me, it's been delightful. I can't say I've ever had so much fun," she confessed. "However, I'm not looking for another heartbreak."

"I understand, Beatrice," I said ready to walk through this door of opportunity. I'd been wondering how I could have the "men leaving" conversation.

"I'm not looking to break a heart. I've had my

heart broken before, at times it felt as if it was beyond repair. But, I couldn't give up on love."

Beatrice shook her head in a way that indicated, *I'm not trying to hear that.* "How did you bear the pain?" She asked. "How did you regain your bearings?"

"I spent a lot of time praying. With time I came to realize that I learned things about God and myself that only a painful heartbreak could facilitate. Instead of trying to find the perfect woman, I decided to present myself for God to perfectly love the woman He's prepared for me, through me."

I took a breath trying not to talk so fast.

"Beatrice, the beauty of my brokenness is that I've learned to love without demanding. My journey has been long. My lessons have been hard. Love has awakened me to greater discovery. Love is my purpose. The person I love just happens to be the beneficiary." I hoped my transparency would welcome her to my love.

With brashness, Beatrice asked, "Just what is it that you know about love? I too thought that I knew love and yet over and over again, love escaped me and left me to die inside, and I don't want to go through that again."

I nodded at her response. She'd built a high wall. "Beatrice, I know love is the greatest gift power available to man and that sharing love is the greatest privilege. Perhaps, it was the *misrepresented ideals* of love that abandoned you and left you to die, not love."

She sat back in her seat, rested her head on the headrest and closed her eyes. As the bus rolled along, we rode in continued silence, each in our own thoughts. I knew there was more, but I was willing to wait for it. Beatrice needed time, and I wanted to oblige her. After all, love is patient.

Finally, she opened her eyes, put her knees up to her chest and faced me. I turned and gave her my full attention.

"For the last three years, I've taken myself out of the *love game*," she said while fidgeting with the silver ring she wore on her thumb. "I painfully recognized that the common denominator in my failed relationships was me. And honestly, I was sick and tired of the me that I had become."

She positioned herself facing me, looking me in the eye and continued.

"I had allowed people and circumstances to alter who I was and even who I wanted to be. So, I took the time to find my way back to myself. However, along the way, I think I began to embrace solitude too much. I think I was even beginning to use it as a crutch. I rationalized that if I let no one in, then no one could hurt me."

I straightened up and looked at her. "Well, I'm not so sure about that plan," I confessed. "I understand the pains of failed relationships, and I too have come to realize that the common denominator was me. You are not alone in this dilemma. I realized that I loved people for who I wanted them to be instead of taking time to know them and love them for who they were. I was expecting them to value me in ways that I didn't value myself."

I could tell she was holding on to every word I said, as I continued.

"Beatrice, I have come to realize no one could hurt me more than I was hurting myself with faulty expectations and requirements that were not mutually agreed upon. I was impatient and didn't pay attention to the 'relational' traffic signals. You know, those that say, 'slow down' or 'stop.' I was like a driver approaching an intersection trying to beat the red light."

She leaned into her seat.

"Instead of paying attention to signs and responding appropriately, I rushed on through the intersection. Unfortunately, I've been ticketed and even crashed. I've paid the price."

She smiled and shook her head. "You have a way with words," she said.

As she confided in me, I saw a peacefulness overcome her.

"Redo, the more time I spend with you, the more I know that something inside of me recognizes something inside of you," she said slowly as if coming to realizations with each word she spoke. "My journey, my lessons and my purpose all seem to have led me here to this place, this time, and these moments with you. If the love that God has for me lives in you, and I'm to be the benefactor, then I'm completely overjoyed."

There were tears in her eyes now as she leaned in close to me and grabbed both of my hands in hers.

"I take back what I said. You are not a *nice* guy after all. Nice is too small of a word for the man that you are."

Shaking her head again and shrugging her shoulders, Beatrice turned towards the window and slowly exhaled.

I was speechless and reveled in the silence that followed.

Finally, we arrived at Ouarzazate. The Hotel, Le Berbere Palace, was no disappointment. The terracotta exterior was like an oyster's shell that preserved a beautiful pearl inside.

I can't wait to explore this place.

The five-hour drive and the emotionally charged conversation with Beatrice left me wired from my fingertips to my toes. Before, calling it a night, I decided to go for a swim to relax. The pool area was spectacular with pergolas, deck chairs, sun lounges, outdoor dining spaces and huge palmetto palm trees highlighted with a beautiful array of LED lighting. The area screamed relaxation.

I dove in. The water was warm and relaxing.

After ten laps the length of the pool, I was 'butterfly stroking' my way back to the shallow end of the pool, and suddenly I noticed Beatrice sitting in one of the deck chairs.

"So, Redo Phelps, are you training for the Olympics?" Beatrice shouted with an inviting smile.

"No, just relaxing. Can you swim?" I asked, as I changed course and swam to the poolside next to her.

"No, I love being close to the water, but I can't swim," she said.

"Great," I responded. "You can come close to the water and not have to swim. I will hold you and let you float. I will not let you go."

"What? Redo Stuart are you serious?" A look of fear appeared in her eyes.

"Well, you've been pretty daring," I said, … Sand Dunning and Camel-back riding. What's one more adventure?" I rested my arms on the edge of the deck. "Come on, sit here and put your feet in the water," I coaxed as I patted on the side of the deck.

To my surprise, slowly she rose still looking hesitant but willing to try. The white lace cover-up dropped.

There she stood in a neon yellow full-body bathing suit.

Slowly she drew near me, carefully sat on the edge and placed her feet in the pool.

"Now, that wasn't so bad, was it?" I asked.

With warm eyes, Beatrice looked at me and said, "I don't know what you are doing to me, Mr. Stuart. My friend won't believe this when I tell her. She has never been able to get me this close to the water. I have never been in a swimming pool."

"Well, technically, Ms. Napal, you are not in the pool."

"Still snippy, huh?"

"Yeah," I said as I moved toward her, took her arms and placed them around my neck, leaned in and whispered in her ear, "let go and trust me," as I gently lifted her from the deck and into the pool. "Now, you are in a swimming pool," I said as she clung to my neck. There we stood face to face.

"Are you okay?"

"Yes," she said doing her best to be brave.

"Now, I'd like to guide you through the water. Turn around," I instructed. "I'm going to put my arms around your waist. Relax, just let the water lift you."

Slowly, I begin to move her through the water, slowly she began to relax and slowly we floated the night away.

The pool was closing. Beatrice and I said good night and headed back to our rooms. I extended the gentlemanly offer to see her to her room.

However, she declined, "No thanks."

Ouarzazate's Hotel, Le Berbere Palace, was indeed 'without noise' or 'without confusion.'

I arrived to my room, put on some music and decided to get a shower. Suddenly, my phone rang, stabbing my ears and interrupting my pleasant reflections. It was my favorite aunt.

"What's up Red?" Red, was my childhood nickname.

"How's Morocco?"

"Hello, 'T', Morocco is growing on me." I sighed, my thoughts going back to Beatrice.

She knew me well enough to know that by the

sound of my voice, I was referring to more than the place.

I could hear her smile on the other end of the phone. "You know what *they* say Red, it only takes one spark to start a wildfire."

"Yes, 'T'," I said grinning. "Whomever, *they* are, *they* got it right this time. I've found love."

"Well, are you bringing it home with you?" She asked with a sassy rasp in her voice.

"I'm not sure what to do with it. Right now, I am basking in the moment."

"Does the object of this love have a name?"

I could see her curling up in her chair, taking a sip of what she affectionately calls her, 'medication' while waiting for my answer.

"Beatrice…" I say, loving the taste of *her* name on my lips. "Her name is Beatrice Napal."

"Beatrice Napal," she repeated with a raspy swag and chuckle.

'T' wished me luck and hoped she would meet Beatrice soon.

SIX

Essaouira [es-uh-weer-uh]

LOVE'S PARADOX

It's day seven. The bus will leave at 10:00 AM. I decided not to go down for breakfast and ordered room service instead. While browsing through the Kuryakyn motorcycle accessories website, I sipped my coffee and thought more and more about having her in my arms.

After a hot shower, I packed up my belongings and prepared for the day's travel.

While walking through the lobby, the aromas of rose and lavender from the spas were stimulating me even more. I was feeling a bit amorous. Perhaps, the six-hour ride to Essaouira will give me plenty of time to sort through what I'm feeling and thinking.

I walked onto the bus and saw her and the empty seat next to her. Knowing the seat was for me, I made my way down the lean isle towards her.

"Good Morning, Beatrice. Are you ready for the road?" I asked as I settled into the empty seat next to her.

Beatrice had a refreshing glow that was accompanied by the sweet aroma from the spa.

"You look and smell wonderful," I said.

Beatrice looked at me smiling. "Thanks, I was feeling tense and decided to treat myself to a facial and massage before the long ride."

As Pierre narrated the unparalleled panoramas while leaving the Mid Atlas Mountains, I could tell that Beatrice had a lot on her mind. "Are you okay?" I asked. "Would you like to talk?"

"Redo, as much as I think about all that we have experienced together, I can't help but think about the unlikeliness of it going much further. You and I live worlds apart. This trip has been an amazing experience, but what happens when day twelve comes and we find ourselves back to our individual realities? You said it yourself; we are both retreating from our busy lives…"

I sat back in my chair, knowing this was coming. I wanted to relieve her of her worry. I trust that God has a plan for both of us and that we are both involved in His plan together.

"Beatrice, maybe it's time to slow down. It took this time and this unlikely place for me to find you. And while our lives may seem worlds apart, they also seem divinely connected."

I leaned towards her. She leaned towards me, wanting to grasp every word I said.

"I knew from the moment I saw you that we were destined to be here - now. I'm not seeking an opportunity or a short-term convenient arrangement. I am seeking the woman God has prepared and sent to love me. I know all too well the misfortune of trying to make relationships more than they are or should be. This trip has become more than a geographical excursion. To me, it's has become more like 'Paradise Lost' and 'Paradise Found.'"

I grasped her hand. "I have dreamed of you since childhood. I lost you when I lost me. I came here to find me, and I found you. I found me in you and you in me. We are woven from the same fabric of love. I don't have the answers you seek. All I know is that today, I have you."

As she looked at me, I could see tears leaving a sad trail down her face.

"Why are you crying?" I asked.

"You move me in ways I've never been moved,"

she said, as she erased the trail of tears from the right side of her face with the back of her hand.

Before she could get to the left side, I gently kissed and then wiped that trail of tears with the palm of my hand.

Beatrice looked at me and said, "I do love you Redo Stuart."

SEVEN

Essaouira [es-uh-weer-uh]

CHANGE OF PLANS

As the tour bus pulled up to Le Medina Essaouira Sea & Spa hotel, I was again speechless. Beatrice was resting soundlessly in her seat looking out the window. We were both still processing our conversation from earlier. I heard what Beatrice said, I felt the same way, but still, I didn't know what to say.

As we walked into the lobby, we were greeted by another spectacular convergence of color and style. A private beach, full spa, four restaurants and a rooftop terrace were among the main amenities. We checked in and decided to call it a day.

As we were about to go our separate ways towards our rooms, I wanted to make sure we had some plan. "See you for breakfast?" I asked.

"Sure," she said, as she turned and walked away.

Victor, the concierge in Casablanca, had done an excellent job recommending and scheduling things for me to do on this tour. When I got to my room, I decided to call and let him know how much I appreciated him.

"Victor, everything has been formidable," I said once again speaking just enough French to get me in trouble.

"Mon Plaisir, Monsieur Stuart," he said.

"I am looking forward to the 11:00 AM Tee Time at the Mogador Golf club," I said.

"Hit them straight," he said with a slight chuckle.

"Is there any other way," I responded as I joined the laughter?

After talking to Victor, I decided to go for a jog along the private beach.

As my feet pounded the sand and sweat ran from my face like rain, the words, "I Love You Redo Stuart," were pounding in my head.

Could this be real?

After my three-mile run, I got a mean green smoothie with plant protein and ginger supplements for dinner. I returned to my room, slightly opened the French doors to my balcony, and recollected on the many lovable moments Beatrice and I had shared.

I soon drifted off to sleep while listening to the treble sounds of the wind and the bass sounds of the waves crashing together.

The morning brought with it an army of seagulls squawking in the harbor and an intense headache. As I rolled over, the shrilling sound of the birds only served to intensify an already severe headache.

Rarely, do I get a headache.

What brought this on? Was it the night air?

These thoughts were secondary to the thoughts running through my head regarding Beatrice and my conversation about the unlikeliness of what we've shared not going much further.

I walked over to close the balcony doors and realized that I was in no shape for a round of golf nor breakfast.

I called the golf club to cancel my tee time and inquire of a refund. Then, I called the front desk and asked them to transfer me to Beatrice Napal's room.

I could hear the front desk say, "Ms. Napal, I have Mr. Redo Stuart on the line, should I transfer him?"

"Yes," she said. I could hear a tad of excitement in Beatrice's voice.

"Good Morning, Beatrice."

"Good Morning, Redo. You don't sound good," she said.

"I don't feel good… got a killer headache," I replied.

"Is there anything I can do for you?" She asked.

"You can give me a rain check on breakfast," I said with a woeful voice.

"It's not raining. You will not get off that easy."

"Now, whose being smart? Don't make me laugh, it hurts," I said.

"I'm sorry, Redo," she said with remorse. "I was hoping to help. Of course, we can reschedule. I do hope you feel better."

After getting off the phone with Beatrice, I took my downtime and rested my head on the feather soft pillows in the room. Two hours later, my phone rings.

"Redo Stuart," I said.

"Good Morning, Mr. Stuart, I have Ms. Beatrice Napal on the line, should I transfer her?"

"Please do," I say.

"How are you feeling?" Beatrice asked.

"Fair to middling," I said.

"Well now, that sounds like you need help." Before, I could respond Beatrice says, "Room 109, right?"

I said, "Right, 109."

"I'm going to bring you something," she said and hung up.

My head isn't pounding as hard now. However, my heart is making up the difference. How will I respond to her being in my intimate space?

I met Beatrice at the door with a nervous smile.

She looked at me and said, "The doctor ordered that you stay in bed under watchful care."

"What doctor?" I said waggishly.

"Dr. Feel Good," she said affirmatively. "I brought you a spinach salad as well as a mixture of ginger and green tea. The spinach leaves are high in water and fiber which will make your body feel great," she said this time with authority in her voice. "The tea will help with inflammation."

 "Beatrice are you an Art Curator *and* a doctor," I asked while stepping aside and inviting her in. Little did she know, I was already feeling good. The sight of her energized my entire body.

"I am whatever it is that you need," she said directly and without hesitation.

After lunch, Beatrice insisted that I climb back in bed as she sat, read and wrote in her leather-bound journal.

I was awakened by what I thought was a dream. It wasn't a dream. Beatrice was sitting next to the bed gently massaging my temples.

It was the dawning of the evening; the sun was going down.

"Wow, I've slept the day away," I said. "What a beautiful sight."

"Yes, the sunset is truly amazing," Beatrice said.

"I wasn't talking about the sun. I was talking about you, sitting next to me."

Beatrice blushed and walked over to the French

doors.

"Open the doors and then come join me," I said as I sat up in bed. I patted the space to the left of me.

Beatrice looked surprised and asked, "How's your headache?"

"What headache?" I replied.

She smiled and slowly walked my way.

The sun was like a blazing ball of fire. Yet, nothing like the passion I felt in my heart for her.

As we sat, and watched the sun tuck beyond the horizon, Beatrice, simultaneously tucked her shoulders beneath mine and rested her head on my chest.

In the stillness of the moment, I softly said, "Beatrice, I loved you the moment I saw you. Now, I love you even more." I paused for a second taking in more of the quiet. "I feel like you are a part of me and I'm apart of you. I'm so happy now that you are here with me tonight. Thank you for taking care of me today."

She lifted her head, look into my eyes and sweetly said, "I would have it no other way."

EIGHT

Agadir [ah-gah-deer]

ABOUT LAST NIGHT

The 5:30 AM alarm on my iPhone startled me, jolting me out of my sleep and waking Beatrice up. As I gathered myself, I was even more startled that Beatrice had remained in my room, in my arms until morning.

"Umm, what time is it," she asked as she sat up and pulled her hair away from her eyes.

"5:30," I said, as I tried to regulate all the "what ifs" that were going through my head.

What if I snored? What if I had some wild dream? What if my amorous thoughts and feeling somehow found their way to her while we were sleeping?

"I can't believe we fell asleep," she said.

"Maybe we didn't," I said attempting to lighten the mood. "Maybe sleep fell on us to keep us right where we were, in one another's arms until morning." I smiled at her, knowing my poetic intentions would make her laugh.

Beatrice looked at me and said, "Really, Redo Stuart? Where do you come up with such stuff?"

She asked as she flung a pillow in my face. "You tend to speak in poetic ways whenever I ask questions."

I caught the pillow, "Oh, you want a pillow fight this early," I laughed. "Besides, I can't help it. I was just born with a loving and deep soul." I threw the pillow back at her, hitting her head and chest.

There was no trace of a headache that had attached itself to me the day before. In its place were vibrancy and vigor. I laughed and felt good as Beatrice and I playfully fought each other with the luxurious hotel pillows. We ducked behind different sides of the bed and crawled cross the tossed sheets to hit one another with the pillows, laughing and enjoying each others company.

Before leaving to prepare for the tour bus departure, Beatrice joined me on the balcony for coffee and some granola snacks from the 'care basket' she brought with her when she came to 'doctor' on me. Her presence in my space really feels good.

Beatrice leaves and I realize, it's day nine.

Where has the time gone? What am I to do with the time left?

The thought of this experience coming to an end makes me lonesome for her. I pushed those thoughts aside and made myself gather my things and head down to the lobby.

Pierre greeted us and gave us a briefing on today's trip.

Agadir is a 3-hour drive. This beautiful resort destination is known for its golf courses, wide crescent beach and a seaside promenade lined with cafes, restaurants, and bars.

My original plan for this Moroccan tour was to play several rounds of golf, perhaps a motorcycle ride along the coast and to refuel before going back to my busy life in Arizona. Now, all I can think of is how can I spend the last three days with Beatrice.

As the tour bus rolled along the beautiful coastline, Beatrice was noticeably quiet. I didn't want our last few days to be silent with questions unanswered.

I looked to Beatrice, her head resting softly on the seat as she starred out the window of the bus. "Tell me about your last relationship," I inquired.

She looked at me a little shocked. I knew she was

not expecting such a question, but the more time flew by, the more curious I got.

"His name was Malcolm and when the relationship ended, I felt I'd never recover. Now I can confidently say that he served his purpose in my life. He showed me who he was, but more importantly, he showed me who I was. I didn't like the me I was when I was with him. Ironically, the things I didn't like about him, were things I needed to address in me. And while I will always have a love for him, I would never be able to ignore the fact that he isn't my soul-mate. Some relationships will mature you if you are open to it. Malcolm broke me down so that I could begin anew," she said reflectively. "Why do you ask?" She sat back waiting for my answer.

"Because I want to know if there is room for me in your life beyond here and now?"

"Redo, this may sound strange," she continued cautiously, "but I imagine I knew you long before here and now. When you walked into my life, my soul leaped with a knowing and anticipation of what I suspect once was, or perhaps what could be. Of course, there is room for you in my life. There is a space that no one else could fill."

Tears are flowing again. This time the tears were

mine.

Beatrice seemed paralyzed as she watched the tears flow down my face.

"What is it?" she asked quietly, as she finally awakened from her trance and pulled me closer to her.

"It is the realization that I've finally come to appreciate the difference in trying to force love and just allowing love to flourish. I have longed for this, for you, for us, for a lifetime."

Perfect love casts out all fear. For some reason, I am not afraid of being transparent in Beatrice's presence. It is as if we are in a world all to ourselves.

As we drove past the 'Hill of the old Casbah,' it is hard to believe that this city was destroyed by an earthquake in 1960; it has been completely rebuilt.

Here we are. Sofitel Agadir Thalassa Sea & Spa.

This place is amazing.

The lobby and various vestibules are appointed with massive white columns. The walls are black and white accented with a plethora of local art as well as mosaic panels. The ceilings are black mosaic tiles with crystal chandeliers. The seating is an interesting duet of white and silver leather. This resort is an artful masterpiece.

While Beatrice and the other guest were checking in, I stopped by guest services and inquired of a beautiful place for dinner. I wanted something quaint and intimate. Tonight, would not be a casual meeting of two tourists who have found traveling companionship. Tonight would be a date.

I can't help but think about last night. She spent the night in my room. While we laid on top of the covers with all our clothes on, everything seemed so natural to us. I felt like Beatrice was my 'missing rib.' Sleep anesthetized us while destiny surgically reunited us.

I loved Beatrice's inaudible confidence. I smiled as I reminisced on our early morning antics.

As we were having coffee on the balcony, I noticed something on Beatrice's face. "Come here," I commanded. She leaned towards me, closed her eyes and puckered her lips as if to prepare for me to kiss her. "You have something on your face," I said.

Beatrice opened her eyes and saw the twinkle in mine. I gently wiped a piece of granola from her cheek. "There, much better."

"Thank you," she said shyly as she quickly stood up. "I guess I better go and get myself together."

"Yes," I said, silently letting her off the hook.

I hated to see her go. I wished I would have removed the granola with a kiss; it would have been much better for both of us.

Guest Services agreed to cater a private sunset dinner on Presidential Bay Front Private Balcony II. I arranged to have a three-instrument ensemble to provide music as we dine. Additionally, I asked that a dozen roses be sent to Beatrice's room with the following note:

Each moment with you has been one to remember.

Would you do me the honors by joining me for dinner?

This isn't a casual request. It's a date.

I'll do my best, not to keep you too late.

Presidential Bay Front Private Balcony II

6:00 PM RSVP -- Redo Stuart

I got to my room and decided to call my Grandmother. I seldom go nine days without checking on her. She is 102 years old and still quite keen.

"Baby, I'll be glad when you come back. Grandma misses you."

"I'll be leaving in three days granny," I said dulled by the wretched reality that my time here with Beatrice is coming to an end.

"I pray for your safe return," she said. She ended the conversation as she does with every conversation. "Be Sweet."

I was wondering if Beatrice had gotten the flowers and if she had read the note. *Would she accept it as an intentional date or would she see it as just a nice gesture from a nice guy?*

Suddenly, the phone on the nightstand rang. The caller ID read, B. Napal – Room 48.

"Redo Stuart," I said with a big smile.

There is a sigh.

"Redo Stuart, you continue to wow me speechless," Beatrice said.

"You sound pretty good right now," I retort.

"Does this mean that you are open to our date?"

"Yes," she said. "I called to say thanks for the lovely poem and flowers. They are gorgeous."

"So are you Beatrice… see you at 6:00 PM."

After I hung the phone up, I realized that I didn't have wardrobe suitable for the evening I'd planned with Beatrice. So, I went back to Guest Services and inquired about a place where I could remedy that situation.

Marchelle, at guest service, recommended Wild Clothing which was conveniently located along the seaside promenade.

"I'll get you a driver, Mr. Stuart."

"Je vous remercie," I said.

"Vous *êtes* les bienvenus, Marschell replied.

My subscription to Rosetta Stone French has proven to be a worthy investment. However, I continue to remind myself that I only know just enough to get me in trouble.

As the car pulls up to the store, attendants approach me and say, "Mr. Stuart we were informed of your needs. Right, this way."

The Wild Clothing store was indeed wild. A diverse range of clothing from sportswear to fine apparel.

After my necessary shopping excursion, I quickly returned to my room, showered and got dressed. The midnight blue double-breasted suit, white shirt, mustard yellow with a crimson paisley tie and the crimson pocket square was perfect. To top it off, I bought a bottle of, "French Smell Good."

Oud Palao Eau de Parfum will forever be a special fragrance for a special occasion. It's combined signature scents of Agarwood, or oud, also known as liquid gold, mingles with rose, vanilla, incense, and cypress. The aroma is intense and absorbing.

I arrived at the Presidential Bay Front Private Balcony II early because I wanted to make sure everything was in order. The waiters and three-string ensemble were in place. The round black marble table was adorned with Versace Byzantine China as well as the Arcades Crystal Stemware and Candelabrum. Everything was magnificent.

The ensemble began to play as I stood looking at the sun dancing on the ocean.

What would I say to her that would adequately convey my thoughts of where I'd like to go from here and the fact that I didn't want to go alone?

Beatrice made the perfect arrival as the ensemble was playing a Stevie Wonder classic, 'My Cherie Amour.'

As she drew within 'earshot,' I began to sing. I am no soloist. However, my heart sings to her. This time, I allowed the words to come out of my mouth, "La la la la la la, la la la la la la... My Cherie amour, lovely as a summer day."

"Hi!" She said softly. Then, "Pinch me," she said. "Is this real?"

"Hi!" I greeted her. "This is as real as I can be," I said and gently pinched her.

I took her hand and led her to our table where the waiter took our drink orders. I could tell that Beatrice still wasn't sure what to make of all this.

"So why is a man like you single when this kind of treatment could get you any woman you want? When was your last relationship? What happened?"

The rapidity of the questions nearly made me choke on the Perrier.

"I am single because I prefer to wait on my Soulmate. I don't engage in the social game of 'wow them until you win them.' My last romantic relationship was 2007. Her name was Rebecca. I guess you can say that I didn't know how to date. I was predisposed to this fairy tale love life that I had created in my head since childhood. I entered the relationship without clear expectations and boundaries. I entered the relationship without establishing requirements that were mutually agreed upon. Consequently, I was expecting things from her that she never agreed to. Am I over her? Yes, it was a season in my life that taught me, you can't make a *wrong* decision, a *right* decision, by making it a *permanent* choice."

Our food arrived just as I was finishing my explanation and I hoped I answered all of her questions. I wanted to stay in this moment. I wanted Beatrice to know everything about me and I wanted to know everything about her.

"Thank you," Beatrice said.

"For what?"

"For everything," she said simply.

After I offered a thanks for the food and the evening, Beatrice and I enjoyed a well prepared five course meal as we watched the beautiful sunset and listened to the wonderful music.

Together, we were in a place above the moon and beyond the skies. We were in spectacular bliss.

"Come here," I said.

"What," she asked uneasily as she removed the white napkin from her lap. "Is there something on my face again?"

"Here, let me help you," I said as I took the napkin, leaned in close to her face and kissed her on the lips. "Now, that's better."

She looked at me and childishly said, "Do it again."

We laughed out loud.

Without hesitation, I did it again.

NINE

Agadir [ah-gah-deer]

A NEW MOON

It is 9:00 PM. The ensemble played their last song as Beatrice and I danced.

I looked out over the balcony; the new moon is shining bright. I tend to recall from my high school science class that the New Moon is when the Sun and Moon are aligned, with the Sun and Earth on opposite sides of the Moon. Even though Beatrice and I are on opposite sides of the world, I feel that we are aligned. Perhaps, she's the Sun and Moon. Perhaps, I'm the Sun and Earth.

"The moon is beautiful," I said.

"Divine," she said as she tilted her head upward looking out over the balcony at the bright moon.

I looked down towards her, eyes glistening like the stars she was looking at. "Would you like to take a walk on the beach?" I asked, trying to extend the evening.

"I would enjoy that," she said as the music diminished and ended our dance. Beatrice looked up at me smiling.

As we got down to the beach, I rolled up my pant cuffs. Beatrice and I both removed our shoes. The cool sand seemingly massaged my feet as we walked. Beatrice and I walked and talked for miles.

After a while, Beatrice spoke up with a question we both knew was coming. "Redo, doesn't it concern you that our work and lives position us worlds apart?"

I smiled at her, "Only if you aren't willing to give me your contact information," I said. "We've spent a lot of time together these past nine days. And yet, I don't have your phone number."

"You haven't asked for it," she said coyly.

We paused for a moment and exchanged contact information. Beatrice reached into her bag and pulled out her phone, unlocking it and handing it over to me. I did the same. I was smiling real big inside. Finally, I get her number.

"Redo, I have a confession."

"What is it?"

She pauses and takes a breath. "Early on, I thought that you might be a gigolo." She looked at me questionably with a worried look on her face of what I might say. I didn't say anything; I just squeezed her hand. I was confident that now she knows I am not a gigolo after the time we've spent together. "Thank you for being a caring, sensitive and deeply romantic man. Every moment with you has put a smile on my face and happiness in my heart."

I wrapped my arm around her shoulder allowing her hand to rest across her chest, still holding mine. "Thank you," I said as we made our way back to the hotel. "Even though we live apart, love finds a way. I would love to keep in touch with you."

"You know, they do say that distance makes the heart grow fonder." She said with raised brows.

"Who are they? Where did they come from? I can't help but wonder," I say in mockery. "Seriously, I've learned not to listen to what they say. I'm going to miss you in the worst way," I said as we stopped to put our shoes on.

As we passed through the lobby headed to the elevators, I felt that we had become closer than close. I didn't want to part with her, knowing our time was short on this trip I never wanted it to end.

"Can I see you to your room?" I asked hoping not to seem anxious.

"You can," she said.

As we approached the door to room 48, I couldn't help but think about last night. As Beatrice handed me the key, I unlocked the door. Like magnets, there was a strong force pulling us to the center of the doorway.

We embraced, we kissed, we –

It was *Irresistibly Something Special.*

TEN

Agadir [ah-gah-deer]

SWEETER THAN HONEY

As I got to my room, I could still feel the magnetism that I experienced while standing in the doorway with Beatrice. While my flesh was indeed weak and wanted to go beyond that door, my spirit was willing to abstain.

I was glad Beatrice and I exchanged contact information. I got back to my room and immediately put it to use.

"Siri," I said, "text Beatrice Napal."

"What do you want me to say to Beatrice Napal?"

"Beatrice, I enjoyed the evening immensely. You were absolutely beautiful tonight. Rest Well. Redo."

"Okay." Siri responded. "You said: Beatrice, I enjoyed the evening immensely. You were absolutely beautiful tonight. Rest Well. Redo." Then she asked, "Are you ready for me to send?"

"Yes, thank you."

I was amazed at Siri's next response. "I'm here to

assist you."

I am beginning to appreciate this artificial intelligence even more.

Moments later Beatrice responded via text:

Redo, tonight is another night to remember. Thank you. Did I tell you how handsome you are and how good you smelled? LOL Sweet Dreams.

I slept soundlessly that night. Little did she know, my dreams are coming true.

Day ten in Africa found me invigorated.

I decided to take an early morning run along the seafront promenade with hopes to catch the sunrise. I stopped at a local café to cool down and have a cup of tea. As the tour comes to an end, I am hopeful of the possibilities of a new life journey with someone to share it with.

This trip was intended for me to relax. And I have. So much so that the course of events has caused me to reconsider what I want to do when I return.

I think I've given all that I have to give to the Corporate world. It's time for me explore my dreams of owning my business, I thought. *My pastoral duties are rewarding; however, I think I will expand those to include international mission trips. There is so much for me to do.*

Being here and experiencing Beatrice reminded me that the First Man, Adam didn't go looking for a woman. When God had finished the First Woman, Eve and had taken the time to prepare the woman for her assignment, He woke Adam out of his sleep and presented the woman to him.

No more sleepwalking for me. The idea of having that woman specifically made suitable for me and waiting until God made her known unto me is energizing.

As I made it back to the hotel, I stopped by the local attraction Kiosk. The Imouzzer & Paradise Valley Half-Day Tour seemed interesting. The weather was perfect.

"Siri," I said. "Text Beatrice Napal."

"What do you want me to say to Beatrice Napal?"

"Good Morning. It's a beautiful morning. Can I interest you in a Half-Day Tour to explore the natural beauty of Imouzzer and Paradise Valley? Redo."

"Okay," Siri confirmed. "You said, Good Morning,

It's a beautiful morning. Can I interest you in a Half-Day Tour to explore the natural beauty of Imouzzer and Paradise Valley? Redo."

"Are you ready for me to send?"

"Yes, thank you."

"No problem," Siri said.

Beatrice replied promptly:

Good Morning. You're up early.

And so did I:

Yes. I went for a morning run.

I smiled as she confirmed her interest.

What time is the tour?

I found myself now anxious to see her again as I relayed the logistics:

Tour Bus leaves from the lobby at 9:00 AM.

Again, she promptly replied:

Sure thing. See you in the lobby at 8:50.

I quickly responded as I made myself ready for the day:

Great! I look forward to it.

Time passed quickly, and once again I was in the presence of Beatrice. As we entered the tour bus, she seemed to have a delighted glow.

"How did you rest last night," I asked.

"Well," she said.

The local tour guide gave us the Birdseye view of the tour which included flowing streams, limestone gorges, rich plantations, and charming villages in the picturesque Moroccan countryside.

The first point of interest was a scenic drive, passing by a Saudi palace and through Aourir, which was nicknamed 'Banana Village' by Jimi Hendrix due to its dense banana groves and the vast quantities of bananas sold on the roadside.

We continued through winding roads and saw the contrasting, colorful landscapes until arriving at the fittingly named Paradise Valley. The deep, palm-lined canyon, combined with a flowing river snaking along its base, creates another excellent photo opportunity.

Beatrice and I took another photo. This time we were both eager. It was as if we both knew that this picture meant that we were together in paradise.

We continued our journey through an abundance of argan, almond, and olive trees before reaching Imouzzer, a small village tucked away in the westerly outcrop of the Atlas Mountains. Beatrice and I meandered along the walkways, souvenir shops, and cafés.

The last stop was Izourki Oufella, a region that is popular for its varied and refined honey. We learn how thyme, orange blossom, and even cactus is used to process the honey. We both loved the honey and decided to purchase an ample supply to have it shipped back to each of our homes. This would be a memorable souvenir that will remind me of how sweet my Moroccan experience has been.

As Geno, our friendly, tour guide headed back towards the hotel, Beatrice and I spotted an interesting place to have lunch along the promenade. We decided to get off the bus and asked Geno if he would let us off at the next intersection.

As we made our way walking along the promenade, we took in all the culture had to offer us. Finally, we found our way back to the Pure

Passion Restaurant. The window seat provided a great view of the people and the marina. As people of various nationalities provided a beautiful landscape, I couldn't help but think of my tour and my time with Beatrice coming to an end.

The menu was a splendid variety of French, Seafood, Mediterranean, European as well as Vegetarian-Friendly, Vegan and Gluten Free Options.

I didn't have much of an appetite. By the way that Beatrice picked at her food, I could tell that she didn't have much of an appetite either.

"What is it?" I asked.

"You've reminded me of a love I used to know – a love that I dreamed of every time I closed my eyes. A love that was genuine, gentle and lasting, a love that until now, eluded me. In the short time I've known you, I now question if I've ever really experienced love. Have I even given it a chance? Did I even know what it was?"

Once again, tears began to flow from her eyes.

"Please, don't cry," I said as I took her hand. "I hear you. I see you. But most importantly, I feel you," I confessed as I wipe the tears from her eyes.

"My head and my heart are at odds because my head is telling my heart that a long distance relationship just can't work," Beatrice revealed.

"You know Beatrice, I recently read a book entitled *Can These Bones Live?* The book uncovers the effects that neglect, abandonment, and abuse have on relationships. There was a chapter in the book that talked about 'maintaining relationships.' One thing the author makes clear is, love will find a way."

"Yes, but what if love isn't enough to bridge the troubled waters of remoteness?" She persisted.

"In this chapter, the author shared an interesting observation of how passion generates momentum and creativity in relationships. Interestingly, he used the behavior of honey bees. There is a lot that we superior creatures can learn from the behavior of insects."

"I hate bugs," Beatrice said as she jerked, quirked and shook her head. "But I'm curious as to what honey bees have to do with relationships."

I laughed and continued, "Get this Beatrice," I said eager to explain. "All honeybees are social and cooperative insects. There are three classes of bees in the colony; they work in concert to complete the complex task of gathering nectar and sweet deposits from plants. They work to build and protect the hive all while modifying and storing the deposits in the honeycomb." I could see the slight confusion grow on her face as she tried to follow what I was saying. "If a queen bee dies, the worker bees select another queen and feed it a special diet until it becomes fertile. The honey becomes a source of food and sustains the bees during the winter months when there are no plants from which to draw nectar."

"Huh?" Beatrice said clearly puzzled. "What are you saying?"

"I'm saying; we don't have to let this experience die because we are going back to our respective homes. Let's find another way to build and protect the hive so that our relationship can become fertile and sustain us through the winter of remoteness."

Beatrice nodded her head. "So, are we in a relationship?" She inquired.

"A relationship," I mused out loud. "The state of being connected." I sat back in my chair and pretended to study her question. "Let me see,"

I said as Beatrice looked on in wonder. "We've eaten breakfast, lunch, and dinner together. We've ridden dune buggies and camels together. We've waded in the water together. We've laughed, and we've cried together. We've slept in the same bed together. We've kissed together…"

"I get it," Beatrice said as she gently nudged me.

"The real question," I surmised, "… is do you want to continue this relationship?" I asked as I gently nudged her back.

"I want to continue to experience all that Redo Stuart has to offer."

"Okay, I choose you to be my new Queen Bee, Beatrice. I will feed you a special diet of God-like love."

I pulled her close, kissed her on the forehead as she said, "I like that author's insight."

ELEVEN

Casablanca [kas-uh-blang-kuh]

NOW WHAT?

After breakfast, Pierre greeted us as we boarded the tour bus for the 4-hour drive back to Casablanca. The ride back was unlike any other segment of our eleven-day journey. It was as if a dark cloud of reality threatened to invade the bright skies of hope I'd felt each time I was with her.

Beatrice didn't say much; however, she wrote a lot. I could see both pleasure and pain in her face as she wrote. Even though there wasn't much being said, there was peace in knowing we were connected.

What had she written in the beautiful leather-bound journal? What's next? What now? What does Redo Stuart have to offer?

My thoughts were endless and intrusive. I decided to finish reading James Patterson's latest novel in an attempt to distract my mind.

As we entered Casablanca, I couldn't help but notice the whitewashed Moorish buildings and the unique mixture of tower blocks and French colonial architecture off in the distance.

However, this time, the effects on me are much different. Instead of unwinding and settling into the tour with excitement, I am feeling an emptiness at the thought… distance, distance, distance.

As we entered the lobby of Le Royal Mansour, Victor, greeted me with a warm welcome.

"Bon retour parmi nous," Monsieur Stuart.

"Merci beaucoup Monsieur Victor," I said with a forced smile.

"How was the Moroccan experience?" Victor asked.

I looked at Beatrice and responded, "Life changing."

"How will you spend your last evening?" Victor asked with examining eyes.

"Together," Beatrice and I said in unison, without thought or consent.

As we checked in, we agreed to get a little rest and meet back in the lobby at 6:00 PM.

There was something about room 913 that made me want to return. As I put my bags down, I remembered the beautiful butterflies glistening in the sun as they gently landed upon the Roses of Sharon in the well-manicured indoor courtyard my first morning here.

This is where I want to spend my last evening with Beatrice.

Here I am in an unlikely place, having met an unlikely person and facing the possibility of leaving an unlikely love. As I stared into the courtyard, I felt the need to talk to her and to talk to her now.

Suddenly, my phone rang. Its high-pitched sound pierced my ears, and pulled me out of my thoughts. It was my brother.

"What's up, Bro?"

"Hey Man," I solemnly said. My brother and I are two years apart but having grown up without a father, he played father and big brother. Needless to say, he took those roles very seriously.

When I was a little boy, he would always tell me that I *fell in love too quickly.* Consequently, I got accustomed to having a broken heart. I here were times he'd shake me and say, "Boy why are you crying over that girl?"

I've had plenty of shaking in my life.

I could hear him shuffling around through the phone.

"What's wrong Bro?"

I slumped down onto the bed, sinking with the mattress.

"Nothing," I said.

He paused and chuckled. "Oh no, you sound lovesick," he said with a dismissing chuckle.

I straightened up. "Well, I'm not sure that I'm sick yet. But I am sure that I've found love."

"Well, Bro, you're grown now," he said without thunder or lighting. Normally he would try to reason with me about the decisions, but this time I knew he could tell how I felt, happy but sad. "What are you going to do with what you've found? Are you going to hold on to it or let it go?"

I got up and started to pace. "I'm in Arizona. She's in Paris," I first stated as I told him about my encounter with Beatrice. "The first time I saw her, the whole room seemingly spun around her.

She was the center of it all to me."

"Wow man, she must be something for you to see her as the center."

"I took every opportunity to get to know her. She wanted to get to know me, too. We just clicked."

"So, has she told you how she feels?"

I paused and thought back to when she told me she loved me. I smiled at the memory as the good feeling of her presence took over me. "Yeah, she has."

After an hour of me going on telling him about my Moroccan experience, he finally said, "You know what they say?"

I stopped fiddling with the lampshade and looked up out the glass doors. "Here you go again. What do they say?" I asked with a dash of sarcasm.

"*They* say, if you find love and let it go, if it is yours, it will come back to you."

"That's crazy talk!" I said. "Who are *they*? Are *they* talking about Pigeons or Love?"

"Man, you are crazy," he said as we both laughed.

"It takes crazy to know crazy," I said before I

thanked him for the call.

"We have all been there. Just trust what will happen, you and Beatrice will figure it out."

"I've got this evening to figure it out. My plane leaves tomorrow at 3:00 PM. I'll call you when I make it home."

"Alright, good talking to you."

"You too." I hung up the phone; my mind went straight back to Beatrice.

TWELVE

Casablanca [kas-uh-blang-kuh]

RULES OF ENGAGEMENT

Feeling a bit restless, I decided to go and get a workout before joining Beatrice in what would be our last evening together in this region.

As I sat in the 90-degree wood-fired sauna, I couldn't help what I was feeling. All of me, wanting all of her, in every way. While at the same time, all of me wanted to preserve all of her in every way.

Past experience has proven that boundaries are for my good. If I truly want the woman God has for me, I must respect His rules of engagement, to acknowledge Him, to love with genuine affection, and to delight in honoring another as I honor Him and as I honor myself.

I returned to my room and got dressed for the evening. As I made my way down to the lobby, I realized that I was back where I started, yet somewhere completely different. I was alone but had someone I wanted to serve other than me.

This trip, this person, this experience has changed my life.

People often say, "It's not good for man to be alone." However, I've come to realize it is best for a man to be with a woman made specifically for him.

I'm not sure where Beatrice and I will go from here. However, I'm sure that we will be forever connected.

Later in the courtyard, we talked about things that we'd both rather not speak of. The possibility of never seeing each other, how far apart we will be from one another. Beatrice leaned into me resting her head on my shoulder as we talked.

"What time is your flight tomorrow?" She asked as we walked through the courtyard.

"My plane leaves tomorrow at 3:00 PM," I said, not ready to face reality. I looked out ahead of us and stared at the endless sky seeing how it connects to the land in the distance.

"When do you leave, Beatrice?"

"In two days," she said.

"I'm missing you already," I said as I looked into her eyes. As close as we were, I could tell she felt the distance already, just like me.

"That's sweet," she said nonchalantly.

I didn't respond. Somehow, I knew that at that moment, her words weren't indicative of her heart.

"I'm sorry," Beatrice said sadly. "I am already missing you, too. I have a way of trying to protect myself from being hurt or disappointed." She tightened her grip on my hand. "Redo, this trip was unannounced and unplanned. I was unprepared. I began this journey hoping at best for an adventure, some downtime, and souvenirs that I could cherish for a lifetime. However, what I found was beyond what I'd ever dreamed I'd find anywhere. I found love."

I smiled knowingly and said, "Now, that you've found it, what would you like to do with it?"

"Tonight, I want to dance with it and hold it until the morning," she said as she smiled back.

As Beatrice and I reclined in one of the courtyard hammocks, hours passed as quickly as seconds. The midnight blue sky covered us like a blanket. I couldn't help but notice her *Mona Lisa* like smile; it was soft and subtle and tired. I couldn't take my eyes off her.

"Beatrice, the wisest man to ever live, King Solomon, once said, two people are better off than one, for they can help each other succeed." Beatrice positioned herself to look at me. "He went on to say, a person standing alone can be attacked and defeated, but two can stand back-to-back and conquer. If one person falls, the other can reach out and help. Two people lying close together can keep each other warm." I pulled her closer. "But how can one be warm alone? Finally, King Solomon said that three are even better, for a triple-braided cord is not easily broken."

"You don't seem to need much help," Beatrice said as the *Mona Lisa* smile slowly vanished from her face into a playful smirk.

"Well, the Lord knows I need help," I said with a solemn chuckle. "This trip and time with you has opened my eyes and allowed me to see that life is more than a dream. The reality of a woman made suitable for me makes me not want to be alone any longer."

"What are you saying?" Beatrice asked with a slight quiver in her voice.

"I am saying I want us more than I want *you*."

"Redo Stuart! What does that mean?" Beatrice said as her sudden jerk nearly sent us sailing out of the hammock.

As I steadied the hammock, I attempted to steady her uneasiness by saying, "It means that all my life I have prayed and dreamed of someone like you. Now that I have found you, I want us, the three-strand cord: God, me and you, more than I want you." I explained as I gently placed my hand on her cheek, turned her face toward mine and look into her eyes. "You have locks that fit my keys, and keys that fit my locks. With you, I feel safe with the doors of my heart being open and allowing my truest self to step out. I can be completely and honestly who I am. I realize the locks and keys are only good for the doors the Lord has purposed for me to walk through. So, I want us more than I want you!"

"Redo, I have no words to describe what I'm feeling and what encountering you has meant to me," she said. "But, I know I am forever changed. When you walked into my life, my soul leaped with a knowing and anticipation of what I suspect once was or perhaps what could be. I have a sense of *déjà* vu, as if this moment in time has already taken place, perhaps a long time ago, perhaps in a different setting."

I jerked and said, "Huh!"

This time my sudden movement and utter confusion nearly sent us sailing out of the hammock.

"Beatrice Napal, what does that mean?"

She grabbed me to keep from falling and said, "It means I feel like I was made to love you."

I looked into her eyes as she looked into mine. We leaned our foreheads together. I tilted my head up and kissed her forehead gently.

THIRTEEN

Casablanca [kas-uh-blang-kuh]

A NEW SONG

It's 6 AM. Beatrice and I had spent the entire night in the courtyard talking, laughing and crying, as the sky, moon and the stars watched us and beckoned for an encore. We never wanted to spend a second apart from each other.

It was clear that we wanted to stay connected; however, we were uncertain how we would navigate this from a distance. There were the obvious ideas of facetime, phone calls, and even the old fashion letter.

Beatrice turned to look at me. "Can I accompany you to the airport?" She asked.

"I would love that," I said genuinely pleased.

As the horizon greeted the awakening sun, I asked Beatrice if she was ready for the requested dance.

"No," she said as she pulled away from me.

"No?" I echoed.

"No," she repeated. "I don't want it to be our last

dance." She said, as tears once again rolled from her beautiful eyes.

Her words were penetrating my soul.

"So, we won't dance," I said as I gently pulled her back to me. "I'll just stand still and hold you until the song ends."

She looked at me, smiled and agreed. "What did you pick from your playlist this time?"

"I didn't," I said as we stood there, I began to sing:

They say there's nothing new
under the sun.

How did they know you'd be the one?

The one who'd see me
when I couldn't see myself.

The one who'd capture me
like no one else.

The one who'd stir all my hopes and dreams.

The one who without music
makes my heart sing.

You are the one…

The only one…

There will never be another like you.

You are the one…

The only one…

The one I give my heart to.

When I look into your eyes,
I can't help but smile.

Realizing that the long wait
was worthwhile.

More than a lover, more than a friend, you're my
soul-mate.

You came into my world
not one moment to late.

You are the one…

The only one…

There will never be another like you.

You are the one…

The only one…

The one I give my heart to.

My most intimate dream
has finally come true.

It's hard to imagine life without you.

Together we'll live in perfect harmony.

You are the one, the only one God made for me.

You are the one…

The only one…

There will never be another like you.

You are the one…

The only one…

The one I give my heart to.

There will never be another… like you.

"That was beautiful. I've never heard that song before," Beatrice said quietly. "Who sings it?"

"Crazy About You," I said.

"Crazy About You?" She asked. "Redo Stuart, are you making that up?"

"Yes, Beatrice Napal, I'm making it up," I smiled. "But I mean every word. It's my heart's love song, I wrote just for you. I am crazy about you."

Time seemingly stood still as we stood beneath the sun basking in the beauty of love. Eventually, time caught up with us.

I squeezed her a little tighter. "I have to let you go," I said in a voice that I didn't recognize, "…for now."

Beatrice nodded her head and we walked arm in arm back to the hotel. I saw her to her room, we hugged and kissed and then I went to mine.

I prepared to leave paradise. My heart was heavy, and so were my legs.

How was I going to walk away from love?

Finally, it was time to head to the airport. I left my room, exited the elevators and proceeded through the beautiful lobby, saying my goodbyes to the friendly staff.

As I approached the concierge desk, I could see Victor and Beatrice waiting for me.

"Merci pour tout, Victor," I said, thanking him in his native tongue.

"Se souvenir de moi," he replied, as he gripped my right hand and patted me on the shoulder. "Je me souviendrai toujours de vous," said Victor.

I knew I'd never forget him or the experience.

Victor pointed at the limo that was pulling up. "Compliments of Madame Napal," Victor said as he motioned for the bellman to gather my bags.

Beatrice beamed.

We held each other's hand as we walked to the limo. With every step, our hands squeezed tighter not wanting to let go. My heart was sad but fluttering with excitement knowing our love would last. Once we settled into the limo, we were off.

EPILOGUE

MORE PRECIOUS THAN RUBIES

Dreams do come true, but, do they have to come to an end?

The limo ride was quiet. I held Beatrice's hand as she laid her head on my shoulder. Without interruption, we allowed our energies to bask in the joy of finding each other.

As the limo approached the airport terminal, I was pressed to speak. My watery eyes looked into hers and as I cleared the lump from my throat, I could only say, "Thank you, Beatrice."

Never had I felt so vulnerable but yet so sure of something in my life. I was sure that I had found that woman described in the Proverbs of Solomon, a woman whose worth exceeded rubies. I couldn't force myself to say, "Goodbye." So, I lean over, kissed Beatrice on the cheek and simply said, "Be sweet."

"You be sweet, Redo Stuart."

"Je t'aime, Beatrice Napal,"

"Je t'aime de tout mon Coeur," she said while grabbing my arm, fluttering her gorgeous eyes and sharing that beautiful smile as I exited the limo.

"What?" I said in bewilderment. I had no idea Beatrice could speak French.

"I love you with all my heart," she repeated.

"You've been holding out on me Lady, Woman, Girl?" I shook my head, stepped outside the limo and said, "See you in Paris."

I winked at her, blew her a kiss and slowly walked towards my departure terminal.

DISCUSSION QUESTIONS

Is love something you seek or something that is given to you?

What do you see in Redo Stuart?

What do you see in Beatrice Napal?

Does their love seem real?

Do you think you can fall in love in only twelve days?

What do you think about Redo's honey bee analogy?

What value did King Solomon indicate a woman has?

What do you think makes a man valuable?

Do you believe in soul-mates?

What is the role of a soul-mate, friend, life-mate?

Is love a spiritual or material thing?

ABOUT THE AUTHOR

Author Ricky Allen has a heart for helping others and is an ambassador for love. Anointed to lead, to teach and to motivate, this Kingdom-minded visionary eagerly gives of his time, knowledge, and heart to offer life-help and hope for all who will receive it.

Allen is not only an author but also the Founder and Sr. Pastor of the Immanuel Family Worship Center, Incorporated of Jacksonville, Arkansas as well the Owner and CEO of RELATE, LLC.

The author's passion for ministry and meaningful relationships color all aspects of his life and create in him a trailblazing spirit.

He is married to Annic Jean Allen. They have five children.

Also By Ricky Allen

Can These Bones Live?

Can These Bones Live?
Workbook/Journal

RELATE, LLC

The mission of RELATE, LLC is to educate, equip and encourage Legendary Living, one person, one home, and one institution at a time in order to maximize contributions to interdependent relationships.

Butterfly Typeface Publishing

Contact us for all your publishing & writing needs!

Iris M Williams

PO Box 56193

Little Rock AR 72215

www.butterflytypeface.com